A Mouthful of Dust

BOOKS BY NGHI VO

Siren Queen

The Chosen and the Beautiful

Don't Sleep with the Dead

The City in Glass

THE SINGING HILLS CYCLE

The Empress of Salt and Fortune

When the Tiger Came Down the Mountain

Into the Riverlands

Mammoths at the Gates

The Brides of High Hill

A Mouthful of Dust

A Mouthful of Dust

NGHI VO

TOR PUBLISHING GROUP
NEW YORK

This is a work of fiction. All of the characters, organizations, and events portrayed in this novella are either products of the author's imagination or are used fictitiously.

A MOUTHFUL OF DUST

A Tordotcom Book
Published by Tom Doherty Associates / Tor Publishing Group
120 Broadway
New York, NY 10271

www.torpublishinggroup.com

EU Representative: Macmillan Publishers Ireland Ltd, 1st Floor, The Liffey Trust Centre, 117–126 Sheriff Street Upper, Dublin 1, DO1 YC43

The Library of Congress Cataloging-in-Publication Data is available upon request.

ISBN 978-1-250-38640-3 (hardcover)
ISBN 978-1-250-38641-0 (ebook)

Our books may be purchased in bulk for specialty retail/wholesale, literacy, corporate/premium, educational, and subscription box use. Please contact MacmillanSpecialMarkets@macmillan.com.

First Edition: 2025

Printed in the United States of America

10 9 8 7 6 5 4 3 2 1

For Cris

A Mouthful of Dust

Chapter One

"What are you eating?"

Rubbing the sleep out of their eyes, Chih squinted at the blur of rufous orange crest and black-and-white-striped wings pecking determinedly at the ground not far from their head. The hoopoe didn't pause until she had unearthed a gleaming white grub, snipping it in two with her sharp beak before devouring one half and then the other.

"Something good," Almost Brilliant said with pleasure. "Better than the ants I found over by the tree. Though you should look there and see what else I found."

"I don't want the ants either," Chih said, but obediently they went to look at the tree their companion indicated.

They were still foggy with sleep, but in the disturbed black soil, Chih immediately saw a white gleam of bone. Frowning, the cleric squatted down next to the tree, brushing the dirt away with a stick. It revealed a few more shards of bone, the ants that Almost Brilliant mentioned, and several scraps of faded cloth.

They picked up the largest bone shard, as thick as the bottom of a clay mug and gently curved. It filled up half of Chih's palm, and they ran a careful finger over one edge.

"It might not be human," Chih said, holding the shard gently, somewhere between nervous and slightly heartbroken.

Almost Brilliant ruffled her feathers, the closest she got to a shrug.

"We were told about this place and the demon that stopped here. The time to be nervous about this was before you accepted the assignment back in Jintao."

"I know that," Chih said, picking at a scrap of cloth. It turned out to be a length of rotted green ribbon, and when they pulled it up, they dislodged the earth to reveal three human teeth.

They were still for a long moment, their mind blank and buzzing. There should be words here, they thought, but right now, they couldn't imagine what those might be. Almost Brilliant, done with her breakfast, fluttered over to perch at their side.

"We commit ourselves . . ." she prompted, and Chih drew a shaky breath.

"We commit ourselves to the virtue and mercy of a thousand hands, by whose grace we pass lightly and without offering harm," they murmured, and then the rest came, the first prayer they had ever learned during their novitiate at the abbey of Singing Hills. They repeated it five times, and on the fifth they bowed their head over their clasped hands.

"I am sorry for what brought you here, and I will do my best to see you on."

Chih wrapped the ribbon, the bone shard, and the teeth into a square of waxed cloth from their pack and put it away. There would be a graveyard at some point, or a temple that would house the remains. It would be better than a lonely tree and a mourning train of ants, anyway.

Chih packed up their campsite quickly, shaking out their indigo robe before belting it tight. They'd lost some weight since Jintao, and the robes hung awkwardly on their frame, sagging over their hips and gaping a little at the chest.

I'll be circling back to the Singing Hills after this, Chih thought, pulling out a ball of glutinous rice to eat as they walked. *Home, where the food tastes right. I can patch up my things and sleep in a proper bed for more than two nights in a row.*

As they came down the slope towards the town of Baolin, however, where a famine demon had scorched the land just eighteen years before, home felt a very long way away.

Chapter Two

According to Chih's notes, the town of Baolin was only famous for three things. The first was the black soil, left after the Goat Sisters had drained the inland sea during the Age of Heroes. The soil was so strong and rich that it could grow a field of leopard melons from one full moon to the next.

Baolin also gave its name to Baolin pork. Baolin pork was slow roasted overnight in a thin dressing broiled from, among other things, macerated melon, bulbs of mountain garlic, and oil pressed from a local bony fish. The dish was sticky and sweet with plenty of imitators all over the world, but a young cook had become the adviser to the king of Zhou with just that single recipe.

Finally, Baolin was known for its famine.

Eighteen years ago, a famine demon came to nest in the valley. Its white plucked skin stretched over its sharp bones like the canvas of a medicine tent, and when it arrived, it drove away the water and then brought too much, sickening everything it touched with mold and rot. It was a three-year famine, as tall as a house. A man who had seen it clearly on a cold and biting night said that it walked sometimes on two limbs and sometimes on four, its clawed wings coming down to help it scutter across the ground. When it looked in his direction, he fell down into a violent fit of pure terror.

In the time since, the man from Baolin was unable to stop the fits. When the fear overcame him, he fell to the ground and shook like a piece of beef in the pan. He traveled the world in search of relief and finally came to the Singing Hills in the hopes of finding a cure in their deep archives. In exchange for access to their records, he told the clerics about his home and what had happened there, and so Chih was sent to Baolin.

As they took the steep road down into the town, Chih wondered if the village of their birth looked like this now, calm and prosperous with no trace of the deprivation that came before. When they were two years old, the Boneyard River had risen out of its banks in a rage. The people took to the highlands, where they ate insects, bark, and grass, and, when even those were exhausted, each other.

There was no doubt that the people of Baolin had

eaten one another. It was what people did in the face of starvation. They had done it in the highlands the year Chih's birth family fled, they did it a year ago during the siege of the walled city of Shengzhi, and they did it after the Battle of the Eight Mammoths more than a hundred years ago. The archives at the Singing Hills abbey, both in the volumes that were stored cooled like wine in the deep caves and in the stories of the neixin in the great brass and ivory aviary, were full of such incidents. Where there was hunger, there was desperation, and eventually, the belly cried louder than the children, or the elderly, or the dead.

On the other side of the river, high up on hills, Chih could see the tall pillars of the graveyard, extending back towards the tree line. The pillars, carved from stone and pointed at the top, marked the deaths of the rich, while smaller ash posts would be dedicated to those less wealthy. They could see as well two broad squat brick markers, used throughout the empire as monuments for too many deaths at once. There would likely be more beyond the rise.

Almost Brilliant perched on Chih's shoulder, her crest tickling Chih's freshly shaved head. She plucked gently at their earrings with her sharp beak.

"You are brooding, cleric," she said, not unkindly, and Chih remembered not to shrug and disturb her perch.

"I was only thinking that hunger leaves scars. Here, at Shengzhi . . ."

"You should be lucky enough to scar. Dead things don't."

Chih started to respond to that, but a flash of motion caught their eye, a young kitten tumbled in their path. She was a startling white, small enough that she couldn't quite fill out the wheel rut she sat in. She was, Chih thought, just old enough to be on her own. At her size, she'd be nothing more than a quick bite for a passing fox or hawk.

The kitten opened her mouth in a soundless mew, and with a sigh, the cleric scooped her up. Once held, the kitten started to purr, and even though Almost Brilliant made disapproving noises in their ear, they tucked the kitten into the opening of their robe.

Baolin was not large, but it was beautiful, the houses built from cream-colored brick and tiled in celadon in imitation of the capital. The stone-paved street was busy with wagons and pushcarts vying for right of way, but there were plenty of shaded plazas out of the traffic, places for people to catch a bite to eat or an earful of gossip. Chih paused in one to smile at a little girl with her hair up in four buns, her thumb in her mouth and a wax tablet in her hand.

Chih waved at the little girl to wait before showing her their bare hands. Then with a pass, they produced the white kitten with a flourish. Clumsy magic, but the little girl's eyes went wide, and Chih held the kitten close so she could pet her tiny head.

"You can take her home if you like," Chih suggested. "She'll be a good mouser, I bet."

The little girl shook her head.

"Our cats will kill her, probably."

"Ah well. I'm new in town. Can you tell me where I can get a good meal?"

The little girl nodded and gestured for Chih to follow. The little kitten, back in Chih's robe, purred, and all together they made their way down the street to a larger plaza ringed with shops. There was a general goods store, a tailor, a barber-doctor's shop with its signature sign of razor and needles, a permanent stone inscribed with directions to the miller by the river, and set close together, several noodle shops with long tables outside, probably for laborers and other folks who needed a quick meal. Chih could see that one was already crowded with a crew of river men, busy with their steaming bowls while their boss delivered a pair of tall barrels to the owner. The broth boiling in the enormous kettles smelled good, but the little girl led them past all of that to what looked like a residential house around the corner, taking them to the back. It wouldn't be the first time Chih had found themself seated at a family table, but the back door had quite a professional little sign on it telling them to enter.

A wooden chime clattered gently overhead when

Chih opened the door, stepping into a low dim dining room where a large group was just clearing out. They jostled Chih going by, calling to one another, hugging and saying goodbye, and when they left, there was a tired but cheerful air to the place, a party just missed. The entire place smelled like roasting meat and the fresh oat grass strewn on the floor, and the little girl bowed formally to them over her clasped hands.

"Please-please have a seat wherever you like," she recited. "I'll go call my cousin."

The girl's careful diction made Chih smile, and they took a seat next to an open window, their belly rumbling. Almost Brilliant came off their shoulder to peck at the condiments on the table, the pot of chili paste, a small jug of fish sauce.

"You know you can get a meal at the local temple," she said reproachfully.

"I'm here to talk with people. Cleric Thien always said that when you want people talking, you should look for people eating, and here, look, people are eating."

The young man who came out from the kitchen was round faced with the shoulders of a bull and a narrow mustache that would be the envy of any dandy in the capital. He looked tired, but he smiled when he saw them.

"Hello, brother, it's good of you to come out," he said, and Chih grinned at him.

"It's cleric, not brother, and I am happy to be here. I have heard a great deal about Baolin pork."

He raised his eyebrows at that.

"We have vegetarian options as well . . ."

"That's a very good thing to have," Chih said earnestly, and Almost Brilliant whistled scornfully, but otherwise held her peace. "But the pork?"

"We have enough left from the party to do you up a good plate. Would you like some broth and greens while I warm it up for you?"

"Whatever you think best, thank you."

He wasn't much more than twenty, they thought, with no memories of his own about the famine, but his parents would have them, if they were still alive, and his aunts and uncles as well. After a famine, mostly no one had grandparents anymore.

The broth when it came was well-strained, almost clear and with only chicken and salt to flavor it; the greens had a peppery flavor and were served raw, fresh enough that Chih found a small worm fallen on the edge of their bowl. They passed the worm to Almost Brilliant, who took it graciously from their fingertips. The kitten peered at the plate curiously, but when nothing good was forthcoming, she curled up on the bench by Chih's hip and fell immediately into a nap.

Chih dutifully made some notes about the food, which was good, but hardly exceptional. As they wrote, however, they became aware of a delicious smell, salty and smoky but above all sweet, and a few minutes after that, the young man appeared with a plate of pork medallions spread in a deliberate fan with a fat nest of buckwheat noodles coiled to one side.

"Eat up," he urged, setting it down in front of them. "It doesn't get better than this."

It had been a long time on dried fish and packets of rice wrapped in waxy leaves, and for a while, Chih just concentrated on eating the famous meal that had been set in front of them. The pork was delicately veined with fat, falling-apart tender and so sweet it had to be eaten a bite apiece with a mouthful of chewy noodles to cut through the richness. A dash of chili paste stirred into the noodles added just the right kind of vinegary heat, and Chih forced themself to slow down before they inhaled the whole thing.

"Are you planning on sharing?" asked Almost Brilliant pointedly.

"I think you can get a meal at the local temple if you're hungry," Chih replied, but they separated out a scrap of pork and a bite of noodle for her which she ate with anthropological interest.

"It's nearly candy."

"That's why I like it. It's amazing."

The young man who had served them looked up from the table he was wiping nearby.

"We're grateful for the compliment, cleric, but did your bird speak?"

"I speak for myself, and I am no bird, but a neixin," Almost Brilliant said, standing up straight. "My name is Almost Brilliant, of the line of Ever Victorious and Always Kind, and this is Cleric Chih of Singing Hills."

He blinked, staring down at Almost Brilliant and then behind her as if he expected some kind of trick, and when he found none, he looked at them uncertainly.

"A neixin?"

"They are memory spirits," Chih supplied. "Companions to the clerics of Singing Hills who share our mandate to observe and record. That is why we are in Baolin, and perhaps we could start our work with your name and your famous pork dish."

"It is Li Shui. I can't tell you the recipe for the pork, unfortunately—"

"Wouldn't dream of asking," said Chih breezily, though of course they had.

"—but I can tell you about the only time we ever told an outsider our recipe. Is that something that you'd want to hear?"

"I think it sounds like a wonderful place to start."

Chih pulled out a stub of graphite and their sheaf of scrap paper, all shapes and sizes and textures, bound along one edge with a strip of glue and saved from dampness by an oiled cloth cover. Almost Brilliant, naturally better equipped to remember than any human, fluttered up into the rafters above the eating area, taking in the proceedings with professional curiosity.

As he spoke, Shui mopped the tables with a damp cloth, picking up the bottles of sauce that had been depleted so they could be filled, neatening the already neat benches. The rhythm of his motions matched the rhythm of his words, and Chih found themself nodding along as he talked.

Chapter Three

So my family has been preparing Baolin pork since before there was a Baolin. My grandmother said that her grandmother said that the recipe was the only thing that survived the wreck of the broadsails clipper *Foxlike Quickness,* and before that we made it for the last Phoenix King, before her kingdom went all to ash.

We came to Baolin, and the first three restaurants that served Baolin pork were connected, by blood, marriage, or foster, to the Lis, so we've been doing this for a good long while.

I was born a year into the famine. My milk name was Green, for my mother's wish to see young plants in the fields again, and to honor my older brother. It was also his milk name and he did not survive.

First my maternal aunt's restaurant closed, which was closest to the river and served crayfish as well as pork. Second, my grandmother's restaurant closed, which was at the center of the town, oldest of all and with a gate that was brought all the way from the capital. I still have the gate locked up in storage, all carved with ducks and boars and peaches, but it would look silly in front of my mother's place here, wouldn't it?

This restaurant, the one you are sitting in, was always the least of the three, not as old as my grandmother's and not as popular as my aunt's. My mother, too, was always reckoned the least of the three head cooks of the family, though she always said she'd rather be a third-best Li than the very best anything else.

The years leading up to the famine were lean, but there are always lean years, just as there are always fat ones. Then the flood didn't come while the insects did, and the famine arrived in earnest. One hot summer day, the people of Baolin heard the boom of its naked wings, and that night, we heard it in the street, chewing on the corners of our houses, seeing what there was for it to eat.

I don't suppose I need to tell you what a bad time it was. My aunt, who lost all her teeth and her youngest daughter, won't speak of it at all. Before my grandmother died, she would tell my sisters and me such terrible things, things that gave me nightmares and made us feel guilty for every strand of noodle and fatty pork that we put in our mouths.

My mother, who died last year, told me this story just once, at my cousin's wedding. It was late, and she never mentioned it again, but my mother was never a liar, even if she kept the truth to herself sometimes.

Nothing grew in the river valley the third year of the famine, nothing at all, so my mother and her siblings had to range into the mountains and the forests, carrying digging sticks and bags made out of old clothes. They must have turned over every stone in the region by the time the trouble was over, and they brought back everything they could to share. Finding grubs was a good day. Finding mushrooms was amazing. Finding arrowroot was a treasured fantasy, and that was what my mother was looking for when she went south on aching legs and burning feet. She meant to spend the night in the forest and go back at daybreak. It was farther than most people roamed, their fear of ghosts and beasts stronger than their hunger. However, my mother was the most junior adult in the household then, who received the last food and the least food, and she was even hungrier than most.

Going south had given her nothing more than some mostly rotted quinces. She had already been caned in the town square for eating some of her forage before she brought it to be redistributed. If the magistrate's men caught her a second time, they would chop off a finger. Guilt would have kept her from eating it better than fear, but she had left guilt at home, and fear lived in the village. She ate the quinces, and she was able to sleep and dream of better food than she had eaten.

She thought it was still a part of her dream when she woke to the sound of laughter, high and wicked. At first, she did not know what it was. She said we ate the laughter in the first year, jokes the second.

If her stomach had been as empty as it was earlier that day, she would have stayed where she was, but the quinces reminded her that she was a brave and curious woman and that a third-best Li is still better than a best anything else. She crept out of her hiding place, and even before she saw a glint of fire among the trees nearby, she smelled the rich scent of roasting arrowroot, spotted with chicken fat and wrapped in leaves to give them savor. The smell was so good and so foreign even after only two years that my mother almost fainted. Instead, she crept closer, moving as quietly as she could.

Just as she came to the fire, and just as she was deciding how best to approach the seated figures so that they might share or barter with her, she was able to make out their shadows against the trees around them, black as ink and sharp as fishhooks.

They were men at first glance, dressed in the finest fashion from the capital, but their heads were those of dead deer, crowned with antlers and with long tongues lolling out of their mouths. There were keen teeth in those dead mouths, and as she watched them in quiet horror from behind her rock, she somehow knew that the teeth were real, but the heads were just things they wore, fitted over their true selves like a man might wear a snug cap.

There were three of them around a knee-high pile of hairy brown arrowroots, enough that you could buy all of Widow Pau's jewels if she hadn't one day decided that they were bright sweet berries and swallowed them.

"These are good, so good," the first one of them laughed, prodding at one of the mashed arrowroots in front of him.

"Good with fat, but better with blood," cawed the next, and the third struck him with a flat hand.

"Better still without your complaining! Shut your mouths unless you want the Great Houshun to come and devour us."

"No, don't say his name! No matter where he is, he comes when his name is called!"

"No, don't speak of him at all!"

"He always knows when the night people talk about him, and he'll come and cut out our tongues!"

"He'll rip open our bellies and eat our guts like candy while we beg him to stop!"

"He will eat us down to the immortal stones in our throats, so that we cannot even return to the eighth hell to lick our wounds for four hundred years!"

They fell about the fire, topping each other in gruesomeness and gore about what the Great Houshun would do to them, laughing and shouting until finally, foolish loud things that they were, the Great Houshun appeared.

My mother was frozen by fear at this point, and so weak from hunger she did not think she could have run if she tried. Instead she watched as the demon swept down from the dark sky, its beak as long as her arm, and the leather of its hairless wings tattered into rags. She said it smelled of rotten grain and that its belly hung like an empty waterskin.

The Great Houshun, she realized immediately, was the very famine that haunted her town, and she watched as it devoured the foolish night people who had crowed so loudly about it. The famine demon tore off their heads, because wits are eaten first when hunger comes, and then their hearts, because they go soon after. Finally it ate their bodies whole, swallowing them down without tasting them, and its belly, for the moment, at least, was full.

She could have let the Great Houshun pass over her entirely, but as she put it, her wits had been eaten, even if her heart still remained.

She stood as the demon sniffed at the traces of gore left on the ground, hoping for more. She could see that some of the arrowroots had been trampled, but the rest the demon ignored, something that gave her more hope than she had had a moment ago.

"Great Houshun, are you full?"

The demon blinked at her, and by the light of the

fire, she could tell that its eyes were faceted like those of the soldier locusts that swarmed from the south. She had never wondered whose soldiers they were, but now she thought she knew.

"I am full for the moment, woman from the river. You can run now, and perhaps I won't catch you."

My mother shook her head.

"I cannot run, for your amusement or my own life, Great Houshun. Give me the arrowroots by your feet, however, and my family and I will spend all our days running from you."

The famine demon looked down at the arrowroots, turning its head from side to side.

"I will be hungry again in a few moments," it said finally. "I will eat them, and then I will eat you."

"What if I gave you something else to eat, something you have never had before?"

The famine demon sat back on its haunches, looking at her with first one eye and then the other. She realized with its eyes set on either side of its head, it could see her with one or the other, but not both.

"Woman from the river, I am the Great Houshun. You cannot give me something that I have never eaten before."

"But what if I *can*?" she asked, and when the famine demon did not eat her immediately, she could see that she had won at least a little while longer on the earth. She began.

"So my family comes from the south seas, where the fish jump into the nets and the birds lay eggs as big as my fist. There's plenty to eat there, and until disaster brought us north, we raised pigs, hogs as big as horses and long enough to nurse thirty piglets along one side. They gleamed like the sun and swam in the sea, and we sent their meat all over the world, to kings and poets and warlords and gods . . ."

She told him about the pigs, and then she told him about the lanky cinnamon trees that gave up perfect curls of bark, and about honey from the hives of strangely docile, strangely red bees. She told him about how the pork was beaten with wooden mallets until it was tender, and how the marinade was painted on in coats, first in one direction and then the other.

That was the recipe until the Li family came inland, and then she talked about having to relearn how to make fish sauce on the river instead of the sea, and how the shaded forests gave up roots that made the sauce thick and then made it brown.

She told the Great Houshun about the first bite and the last one, and the way a piece of fluffy white bread could be used to sop up all of the sauce, and how a ghost of the meal, in the bones and the scrapings from the pot, could be used to dress a bowl of noodles for the next day.

Under the dreaming eyes of the famine demon, my

mother told it how to make Baolin pork, not just what we do in the kitchen but why, and the demon understood that no human who was not part of the Li family by blood, marriage, or fosterage had ever been told such a thing.

Great Houshun settled down next to the dying fire of its meal, and even if its stomach hung limp and slack underneath it, it made no move towards my mother.

"And when you ate, you were full?" it asked finally, and she nodded.

"Always, Great Houshun."

She waited, and after what felt like forever, the demon came to its feet, and with a great thunder of its wings, it soared away from her, full of something it had never had before. My mother trusted the quality of her family's Baolin pork, that even the dream of it could fill up a famine demon, and she had won her bet.

After the sound of the famine's wings disappeared in the darkness, my mother's knees gave out, and then she could crawl to the arrowroot. She didn't dare bring back one that had been cut, but there was one that had fallen aside when the original owners were eaten, still wrapped in leaves and soft and rich with chicken fat.

She touched it, she smelled it, she looked at the soft white flesh and the gleam of the fat for what felt like days before she finally ate it. She knew that when she did eat it, it would be gone too quickly, so she kept it as long as she could.

Then she came back to Baolin with a tattered bag full of arrowroot under her arm, and as she had promised Great Houshun, she and her family spent the rest of their lives running from it.

Chapter Four

Chih tilted their head to one side. They had ended up behind the curtain leading to the kitchen, sitting on an upturned wooden crate as Shui reduced a rack of pork ribs to manageable cuts of meat. The meat went into pans to be dressed and then roasted, and skin and bones he tipped into a pot of boiling water to make broth.

The kitchen was one that could be found throughout that part of the world, with wide sturdy tables for fast butchering, an oven that stretched along the length of one wall, and pans large enough that Shui's little cousin could use them for a boat. The honey was kept in sealed jars and marked with the chop for the hives at Cu Chi, and dark bottles of fish sauce lined one long shelf like soldiers. A hog head watched over all this from a wooden block; it would eventually be skinned for the tender cheek meat and then simmered whole. To Chih's eyes, it was of a normal size and shape.

"Does your honey really come from red bees?" asked Almost Brilliant, who had apparently been thinking along the same lines as Chih.

"Do I look like I'm serving the Empress of Wheat and Flood?" Shui grinned. "Of course it doesn't."

That was the end of the story then, and Chih closed their book and shook out their sore hand. They wondered whether the demon had been sated with dreams or lies. Demons were known to eat both, but the particulars were still hotly debated in academic circles. The rest of the world was usually too relieved to have survived a demon to worry much about it one way or the other.

"I'll be here in town for some little while," Chih said, putting the book back in their bag. "I was wondering if you could recommend somewhere to stay."

They must have put the right emphasis on the words, because Shui looked up from the cutting board twice and then a light blush appeared over his cheeks.

"Well, there's the boarding house off the main road, of course. It's better than the inn if you're staying more than a night or two . . ."

"Ah. All right."

". . . but you could also stay here if you like. We have a spare room upstairs, and my cousin is going to be staying with our aunt for a few days to work on her knife skills. I wouldn't mind the company."

"Oh, well, that sounds good," said Chih with a grin. "I'll just—"

There was a clatter at the door, and Almost Brilliant hooted with alarm, flying up into the rafters. Shui frowned, moving towards the door with his heavy cleaver still in his hand.

"Some of the barge crews get rowdy when they put in," he muttered, and Chih followed him into the main room.

"We were told that a cleric came here," said a man in painted leather armor, and Chih blinked.

There was no hiding their robes or their shaved head, so Chih stepped forward with a frown. Out of the corner of their eye, they saw Almost Brilliant slipping from the kitchen to the rafters in the dining room, and they were grateful she made no sound.

"That would be me. How can I help you?"

There were four men total in the front room. They had the serious looks of people who were paid to guard very little most of the time, and Chih stood up a little straighter, coming around Shui to stand apart from him.

"We are the household guard of Magistrate Liu. Your arrival was made known to the magistrate, and he expects you to come and stay in his house."

"Ah, I see," Chih said with a slight smile. "Well,

that solves one problem for me. When will the magistrate expect me?"

The head guard glared at them. Chih assumed that it must be irritating to have his veiled threat seen as nothing more than a polite invitation.

"Right now."

"Well, that's very fine. Li Shui, thank you for the meal. I hope to get back at least once more before I leave Baolin."

Shui looked concerned, but not panicked, which was something, at least. He murmured something polite, eyes sliding between Chih and the guards, but he didn't interfere as Chih shouldered their framed pack and followed the guards out. They did not glance up at the rafters, where Almost Brilliant was likely hunched down and doing a very good imitation of a clot of dust.

Clerics were welcome almost everywhere they went. Most people didn't have problems with someone who could bless the local crops and tell a good parable in exchange for some rice and steamed vegetables. The clerics of the Singing Hills, however, were stranger than most, with their deep archives and the long memory of their neixin companions. They recorded and they remembered, and it made them few friends among people in power.

Chih kept their face calm, smiling at the people they passed in the street, treating it all as if it were another day doing the work that they were trained to do. Somewhere above them, Almost Brilliant would be marking this as well, where the guards took them, who saw, who looked away, and who seemed worried or angry. If worse came to absolute worst, it would only take Almost Brilliant two days to fly west to the outpost held by the Sisterhood. The Sisterhood had long ties with Singing Hills, and if they were called, Chih's only job became to stay alive until a representative arrived.

"Yes, even at the cost of your work," Cleric Thien had said. "Remember that your mind and your body are records as well, unique and irreplaceable. You can always write more, and you will if you just remember that."

The magistrate's manor lay behind a tall wall of the same cream-colored brick that was found in the town. Behind the wall, the house was created in the Anh fashion, low and sprawling with elegant raised wooden walkways between the buildings. The gardens were tended with a ruthless efficiency, not a blade of grass or jade boulder out of place, and the only bright color came from the black-hearted red poppies that grew along the pathways.

The guards escorted Chih to the main receiving hall, and after one had gone forward to announce them, they were led in, two guards in front and two behind. Chih kept their shoulders back and didn't bother to hide the fact that they were taking in their surroundings with interest. The magistrate already knew what they were. There was no reason not to do their job.

The magistrate knelt on a raised platform in front of a silk screen painted with the characters for *prosperity* and *justice.* His face was as hard and still as stone, just a touch of dark makeup at his eyes and at his temples to give him a distinguished air. From Chih's vantage point, the only thing that made the man look a little less like a statue was his knuckled hand on his knee, adorned with jade and onyx rings. The hand closed into a fist and then relaxed again, as if the owner was unsure, but then resolved to be sure.

The guards bowed and stepped back, and Chih bowed as a cleric did, hand over their heart and almost as low as they could.

"Who are you, and what is your mission in Baolin?" demanded the magistrate. His voice was a deep boom, but there was an uncertain quaver there, that of a man who was sick or old or afraid or all three.

"Honored magistrate, I am Cleric Chih from the Singing Hills. I was sent by my order to record the stories of the people here."

"You came to pry into the bad days, the famine," the magistrate said.

"Among other things, yes, my lord."

The magistrate half-rose as if he wanted to flee, and

then his hand clenched as if he was pained. Chih wondered if they would be taken to the edge of town and told to leave, or put on a barge and not allowed off until they were in some distant river town. Or perhaps it would be something that began as one of those things and ended much worse.

"Why did you not come here first?" he demanded finally. "I am the magistrate here as my father was before me. My family has overseen the care of Baolin since the reign of the Nameless Emperor."

"I was hungry, my lord," Chih said, and they could almost feel Almost Brilliant tweak their ear for that little bit of disrespect. "I promise you, I only stopped to eat before I came looking for your house."

"And your bird. Your little spy. Where is it?"

"My companion lost interest in my dinner, and likely flew off to investigate the local varieties of gnats and worms that you have by the river. She'll return before too terribly long, I imagine."

"Captain?"

The man standing beside Chih nodded.

"We saw no such bird, sir," he said. It was more likely he forgot to look and was now grateful for the excuse.

"Very well. We have an aviary where my wife once kept parrots, and you shall see to housing your bird there."

"Of course, sir," Chih said easily. The aviary at

Singing Hills was brass and ivory, but it was open to the sky—there was no other cage a neixin of Singing Hills would tolerate. With any luck, however, it wouldn't be a concern. Most people had never realized how difficult it was to catch one specific small bird, especially one as clever as Almost Brilliant.

Chih's placid acceptance seemed to calm the magistrate. His hand on his knee relaxed, and perhaps the barren line of his mouth smoothed a little.

"Quarters will be prepared for you as a guest of this house, and you may conduct your . . . examinations in the little listening chamber."

Chih smiled as if this was delightful news and bowed again, even as a growing unease prickled at the back of their neck.

"Thank you, my lord. I and my superiors in the Singing Hills appreciate your charity and your courtesy."

Magistrate Liu inclined his head slightly, acknowledgment and perhaps some relief.

"Tonight, you will dine at my wife's table. We will certainly offer you better than what you will find in town."

When Chih was shown to their room, a small chamber that smelled of stale fabric with only a single high window, they knew it for what it was. There was a chair for a guard just beyond the sliding door, and all the way down the hallway, the floor creaked like a net full of sparrows, warning in case they should try to flee. They set their pack down, and after the door closed behind them, a full-body shiver traveled from between their shoulders to their knees, striking them so hard that they sat down on the floor.

This could be very bad, Chih thought blankly.

It could be, and the small room with its high lonely window recalled the stories that were kept as faithfully as all the others about the clerics who had died in the course of their duty. The abbey held that the truth would come out anyway, whether it was discovered ten years later or a hundred. The truth was no comfort to the dead, however, and Chih took a deep breath.

I will be careful, I will be clever, and I will tell the abbey all about this when I get back there.

There was a brief rustle at the window, and Chih looked up, hoping to see a familiar winged form there. Instead there was a flash of white, and then a flailing furry shape dropped down from the window, its fall cushioned by Chih's pack.

It was the white kitten from the village, and she peered up at Chih, opening her tiny mouth in an invisible mew.

"Oh, little dummy," Chih sighed, scooping her up and cuddling her against their chest. The kitten, content once more, purred like a hornet, and then leaped onto the floor, nosing around the pallet that had been laid out, the rag rug on the floor, and the storage boxes left piled in the corner. Seeing how unconcerned the little animal was made Chih feel a little better, and if they were feeling better, that meant that they could work. For someone Cleric Yu-ching had once called the laziest rock in the quarry, it was a surprisingly bracing thought.

I am a guest, after all. No reason not to act like one.

They pulled some of the wooden storage boxes close to the window so that the kitten could climb out when she wanted to, and then took some supplies from their pack.

The guard on the other side sat up with a startled grunt when Chih opened the door.

"I am settled in, and now I would like to be taken to the little listening chamber. There's plenty of daylight left, and I can spend it working."

Chih paused, considering.

"Have you always lived in Baolin?"

He nodded warily, and Chih smiled, nothing false about it this time. The guard was in his thirties, they figured.

"Oh, then you must remember the imperial procession of the Empress of Salt and Fortune," they said cheerfully. "She came through some twenty years ago on her way to Ue County. Do you remember that?"

The guard looked surprised.

"I do," he said, and inwardly, Chih cheered.

"Good! Then you can show me where the little listening chamber is, and I shall take your account."

"My account?"

"Of course," Chih said. "Who else will tell me what you saw as well as you could?"

Chapter Five

The walls of the little listening chamber were doubled and stuffed with horsehair and dried moss between them, deadening every sound in the room. They were common throughout the empire, the conceit of the rich and paranoid, and as such, many of them had one extra feature: there was at least one place outside the room where someone could stand and hear everything that was said thanks to a system of tilted copper pipes and angles.

Chih thought it was a rather overdone precaution. It was unlikely that they would get anything useful on the magistrate's property, not when he seemed so resistant to any mention of the famine.

As it turned out, they got more than they thought they would. The guard, Dong Hai, had a lineage in Baolin that Chih suspected went back further than the magistrate's own, and as far as the Singing Hills were concerned, it was no less valuable.

Hai was only ten when the procession of the Empress of Salt and Fortune came through Baolin, riding tall on the back of a mammoth, and her attendants passing out small boxes of black salt to the admiring populace.

Through the curtains of Empress In-Yo's carriage, Hai caught a glimpse of her famous profile, flat compared to the faces of the native Anh people, slightly dished, and he remembered how they had served her a steaming bowl of Baolin pork, which she had eaten as eagerly as any traveling merchant or sailor. The royal procession bled money into the town in exchange for meat, fish, noodles, and adoration, and when the empress moved on, the people of Baolin had to eat skinny chickens and sour sorrel for months until they could replenish their stores.

Hai shyly showed Chih the token the empress's attendants had handed out, a brass coin with a hole through it. On one side, a beautifully stamped procession of mammoths marched around the edge, and when they flipped it, they read the unofficial motto of the last empress's reign: *In winter, fate. In family, victory. In loyalty, all.*

Chih, who knew something of the reign of the last empress, ran the pad of their thumb over the edge of the coin before returning to it to Hai.

"The records of the old empress's reign speak very well of her journey to Ue County and the hospitality she encountered on her way. Did she send any favors back after she had returned home to the capital?"

"During the first year of the famine, she sent fish," said Hai with a wry face. "They were small and half-mashed by the time they got to us. In better times, they would have been fertilizer."

He shrugged.

"My grandmother learned to cook them a hundred different ways, but they never tasted any different or any better. Later on, we would have been grateful even for that, but the empress only sent that first lot. I still eat that fish in my bad dreams."

"Thank you for your story," Chih said with a smile. "I have it written here, and I will read it to my neixin when she returns. Between the two of us, your account will have its place in the halls of the Singing Hills forever, or as close to that as we can manage. Is there anyone else here who knows something about the history of Baolin? It doesn't have to be a scholar or a cleric. I want to talk to everyone."

"My grandmother, she sews for Madame Liu. She was here when Lord Kang chased the white deer across the continent. She says he went straight through the garden in the back, and the old pond is his footprint filled in with water. Would you want to talk to her?"

Lord Kang was a sun god, less worshiped than placated, and never revered. He chased a white deer, or a wounded hound, or the most beautiful boy the sun had ever shone on across the world, until the white deer drowned, or the wounded hound died, or the boy went to live with the dragon king of the western sea and Lord Kang became the Kang Mountain in his grief. Most everyone had a story about Lord Kang crashing through their vegetable garden or barley field. Chih smiled.

"Would you ask if your grandmother is willing to come? Tell her to bring any of her friends who might have something interesting to tell me."

Chih organized their papers, taking some notes on the room and the day, and by then, Hai's grandmother came up to the door, eager to share her story about Lord Kang and her family's recipe for making salted whiskered cod edible.

She brought her friend Sui with her, older yet and nearly blind. Sui had a story about the night a girl with eyes painted on her eyelids had appeared at the gates. The strange girl ate all of Sui's dinner, and then, tipsy on fizzy plum mash, tapped her woven basket and told them how she carried in it a curse that could bring down a king. Sui gave her a pair of sandals, and the girl left behind a bottle of uncooked rice that immediately went missing. During the worst year of the famine, Sui heard the bottle giggling in a cupboard that she opened every day, and that rice saved her youngest granddaughter, Hai's wife, from death's door.

Sui's nephew, Pi, was the town's head mason, at the magistrate's house to look after cracks in the brick and to visit his aunt. He did not want to talk about sun gods or strangers carrying curses, but he did tell Chih about the thin cookies they made with clay when things got very bad. The cookies were baked in the small oven at the masons' meeting house, thin as the blade of a trowel, pale and round as the moon.

"They tasted a little salty, and if you held the dust in your mouth for a little while, you imagined that it grew sweet," Pi said. "We made them by the dozens and sold them for almost nothing. We all knew they were just dust."

Chih licked their lips, imagining the snap of the cookie between their teeth, the puff of dust settled over their tongue.

"But people bought them anyway."

"Of course," Pi said, looking up in surprise. "There was barely anything else. One woman ate so much dust her belly burst, and we saw that her stomach had shrunk to the size of a plum."

Chih wondered how terrible it might be to ask to try one of the dust cookies, but the door rolled open, revealing a bowing servant and letting in a crisp breath of evening air. Chih hadn't realized they had been working for so long.

"Honored cleric, Madame Liu sent me to fetch you for the evening meal."

“And so I am fetched,” Chih said wryly. “Thank you for letting me know.”

They gathered up their things to follow, nodding their thanks to Sui and Pi.

Laughing bottles of rice and dust cookies. It was like getting a picture of a thing by angling mirrors around corners rather than looking at it straight on. It was still better than nothing.

Chapter Six

The dining hall of the magistrate's house was narrow and spare, much like Madame Liu herself. She was a small woman who gave the impression of being tall, and she knelt at the head of the low table as if she had a spear for her spine. Her hair was iron gray, her lips painted a demure lilac, and she wore no jewelry except for four grass-green jade bangles, two on each bony wrist. The bangles chimed gently as she presented the food, the only sound in the room.

The meal, to Chih's surprise, was entirely vegetarian. There were strips of long mushrooms delicately sautéed in wild garlic, a sweet tamarind soup, and small balls of minced vegetables rolled in arrowroot flour and fried in oil.

It was like a luxurious version of what Chih might have received back in Singing Hills, and when they thanked Madame Liu for her hospitality, they were being utterly sincere. It had been prepared with expertise, and Chih realized that it was not just a courtesy to them.

"The magistrate's household has been strictly vegetarian since the bad days," Madame Liu said. "The promise to be so was a sacrifice to bring back the crops and the water."

Her voice was so bland that Chih wondered if she was hiding a certain resentment behind it. To live in the town that was known for a famous pork dish, and to spend almost twenty years eating nothing but vegetables, it seemed as if the magistrate's wife must have something to say about it.

The meal finished with a small dessert of buckwheat dumplings pressed with candied fruit and then drowned in a thin sugar syrup.

"That is one thing you do not miss when you give up meat at least," said Madame Liu with a faint amusement. "You do not lose sweets."

"I saw the Ue County chop on some of the sugar barrels that were being delivered in town this morning. Has Ue County always shipped to Baolin?"

The answer, of course, was no, not with the imperial blockades that went up after Baolin's bad luck. Famines were contagious, and Ue County was fanatic about its quarantines.

Madame Liu was silent for a long time, and when

she finally deigned to look at Chih, there was something distant and disapproving in her eyes.

"Your tricks are perhaps good enough for servants and laborers. It is an embarrassment to try them on your betters."

Perhaps it was, but Chih only tilted their head slightly.

"It was only a question, Madame Liu."

"Why not ask what it is you really want to know? My husband is not here to stop you."

Chih realized that whatever Madame Liu was going to tell them was going to be a lie. Perhaps there was one lie at the core of it all, or perhaps the lies hung off the story like gems buried with a corpse. It didn't matter. The truth, however, was that this was the story that the Lius wanted to tell, and obligingly, Chih pulled out their notes.

"How did the famine affect your home, Madame Liu?"

Madame Liu was still for a moment, gazing into the dregs of her dessert dish as if she could scry something in the milky syrup leftovers. Perhaps she could, because she began to speak.

Chapter Seven

Five years after I married the magistrate, I awakened in the unluckiest hour of the night to the beat of powerful wings.

The wealth of my family in Shouhan came from the rearing of prize hunting raptors. Before I came to Baolin, I helped my mother tame down the fury of speckled northern eagles until they would strike where they were told at least eight times out of ten. The boom from a northern eagle's wings could stun a wild dog. The wings I heard that night, their size and their weight, I knew could stun a mammoth.

I ran past the screens around my sleeping area, joined in the corridors by my maids, and then, a moment later, by my husband's accessory wife Deiyi, and her young daughter.

When a great weight settled on the roof above us, the maids wanted to run out into the yard, to seek cover in the other buildings, but Deiyi and I calmed them and kept them still. I remember Deiyi slapped one girl who had gone hysterical, thrusting her at two others and ordering them to keep her still. She was always a sensible woman. Running out into the open would have made us targets. We waited to see if the thing would peel back the roof to eat us. It paced above our heads, its claws clattering on the green tile. In the morning, we found dozens of those tiles shattered on the ground in front, but the thing did not come inside that night.

Instead, it went down to the village. We learned in the days and months to come that it sickened the trees, turned the fresh green twigs a sickly yellow. The buds gave off a cloudy fluid that smelled of rot. The river refused to flood, and what water did come down was silted and salty, enough to let our crops sprout before they died but not much more.

The first year, my husband opened up the granary reserves. The rations were small, everyone grumbled, but it was enough. It might even have been enough to keep Baolin all three years, but soon, the reserve was tainted. The stores had not been kept dry enough. The older bins had been allowed to go to slime and rot. The mice who raided those bins died of it, and in the end, it had to be burned.

My husband hanged the granary keepers. It was a mercy; the people were already hungry enough to do worse. Afterward, the bodies were burned as well.

Later, the people of Baolin would have called that a waste, but that was early yet.

In two years, things were different. Here at the house, we locked the gates. The people accused us of having vats of pickles buried under our foundations and fat carp in the secret depths of our ponds. The buried vats and ancient carp were of course long gone by then. Instead, we did our best to nurture something that would sustain us in the garden houses. Some of the seed specimens the magistrate brought back from his youth in Zhan sprouted after years folded in cotton. They survived in the heat of the garden houses, pollinated with my finest makeup brushes and tended more carefully than the few children we had left.

It was never enough, though we had a few triumphs. In the midst of the famine, everyone in the household received a mouthful of gleaming black rice, cooked to perfection and salted with salt from Ingrusk. Once, we grew a pot of clover, and we spent the afternoon sucking the droplets of nectar out of the tiny petals.

Everyone inside our gates was grateful because they knew worse waited for them outside. We boiled the books so we could eat the glue, and one winter day, I went looking for leather mittens only to find that a guilty maid had eaten them as well. We were dying, but slowly, and compared to how quickly they died in the town, it was almost tolerable.

The third year, Deiyi's daughter died. We went to

bed early after drinking cups of hot water to quiet our bellies. I woke from a slow and stupid sleep to find the little girl dead and Deiyi filling the halls to bursting with her dry shrieks of grief. Her daughter's milk name was Orchid, and she was the last child to die from the famine in this house, though of course we didn't know it at the time.

Deiyi refused to put Orchid down. She was little more than a bundle of sticks wrapped in a silk gown by then, but Deiyi swore and cursed like a demon herself when we tried to take her away.

Finally, I ordered two guards to hold her while I and my women pried Orchid out of her arms. When she was parted from her daughter, she howled and then fell to the ground, her arms wrapped over her belly. Since Orchid was born, they had never been apart, and seeing Deiyi without the shy little girl at her hems or hanging on to her hips was a terrible thing. When I took Deiyi into my arms, she was only bones.

She kept asking *why,* and no matter what she meant, I had no answers for her.

We put Orchid underneath the house where it was the coolest. We would bury her the next day, but in the night, I was awakened by the sound of people moving beyond my screens. My maids were gone. The only person who was still with me was Deiyi, insensible to the world after I had given her a sleeping draught.

I rose up from my pallet, and somewhere over the

town, I heard the wings of the famine beating distantly in the sky. I could hear it most nights, but perhaps it sounded closer.

Then as now, the kitchen is set against the rear wall of the compound. It stands alone, and so I followed the path the servants took to bring our meals to us in the main hall. The lanterns were cold, but there was a thin glow coming from under the door. The oven was lit, and as I stood at the closed door, I heard the sizzle of something striking a hot oiled pan.

I had never known that I knew that sound so well. It was only after eating borage, flower and leaf, straight off the stalk, after boiling glue and drinking what came of it, that I understood. I had not heard that sound in months, and my mouth filled with spit. My body remembered real hunger, not the strained ever-present hum that had come to live in my bones.

I listened to that sizzling sound as if it could nourish me. I did not move. My hand came up to knock and couldn't. My mouth opened to call for the sleeping guards, but didn't.

They must have seen me through the shuttered windows. I had made no secret of my approach, and I had not tried to hide myself.

Finally, the door opened, and my favorite maid, the one who could always paint my eyebrows perfectly and made us laugh with her songs from the city, appeared. Her face looked no different from when she would ask if I wanted lilac or rose that day for my lips.

In her hand was a steaming bowl. The smell that rose up from it brought tears to my eyes, and only five years as a magistrate's wife and twenty-five years before that as the daughter of Shouhan's finest raptor trainer kept me from lowering my face to eat it.

My maid handed me the bowl and a pair of ivory chopsticks capped with silver tassels. I had forgotten how heavy good china and ivory could be in my hands. Then she closed the door, and I sat down on the stone step to eat.

Chapter Eight

Through the telling of her story, Madame Liu's voice had not wavered. She had barely blinked. Chih noted that as well, and their hand paused over the paper. They hesitated. Madame Liu took pity on them.

"You want to ask me how she tasted."

Chih actually knew. The archives at Singing Hills held thousands of famines, wars, tyrants, and outdated medical beliefs. It was something of a rite of passage for the teenage novices to venture into the archives at night and find the worst of the worst, the tortures and atrocities and horrors that in the end were so depressingly common. Everything and nothing was a surprise for a historian, and Chih knew that starving people had compared the taste of human flesh variously to pork, to chicken, to veal, and to young fawn.

"I want to know how she tasted to you," they said carefully.

For a long moment, Madame Liu was quiet, and

Chih thought of her on the doorstep of the kitchen, listening to the sizzle of the hot pan.

"She tasted like smoke and fat and salt. She tasted like getting to live a little longer, and so she was delicious."

Chih nodded, wishing that Almost Brilliant was here with them. They could write down the words, but Almost Brilliant would recall the glassiness in Madame Liu's eyes, how she worried at the rings on her hand, and how she looked down at the bowls at the table as if wondering why nothing had tasted like that since.

"Thank you," Chih said, and after a long while, Madame Liu inclined her head gracefully to them.

"Let that story stand for Baolin, if indeed anything must. It was a terrible time, and when those who lived it die, it should be forgotten."

Chih bowed from their knees to Madame Liu and rose. As they were turning to leave, something occurred to them.

"What happened to Deiyi, Orchid's mother?"

"A spite suicide, I'm afraid. She cast herself down the well to poison it a few weeks after her daughter died. She is buried in the graveyard east of Baolin. She could not be buried in the family graveyard after that, of course."

"Of course," Chih echoed, and then left before they could be accused of insolence.

A guard they didn't know escorted them back to their chamber. Chih stowed their notes away in their pack and stretched out on the pallet, staring up at the rafters.

If that is what she is willing to tell me, what are she and her husband actually hiding?

The night had grown old, and Chih was almost drowsing off when a shout went up. An orange light came through the small window, and for a moment, Chih thought there was a fire. Then they realized that lanterns had been lit, and the household staff was dashing around the compound, peering at the ground. Some were dressed and some were in their sleeping robes.

Chih opened the door, startling the guard.

"What's going on? What are people doing?"

"Nothing that matters to you. Go back to sleep."

His face was hard and closed, and Chih went back into their room, closing the door after them. Out the window, people were still dashing around, and into all of that came the magistrate and his wife. The magistrate's face was contorted into a grimace, and his wife hung on to his sleeve, though whether she needed the support or she was trying to hold him back, it was unclear.

"Find it!" he shouted. "Find it at once!"

Chih felt their stomach sinking, and then one of the servants rushing by said something hasty to their companion. The words that reached Chih were *white cat.*

Oh no . . .

Chih sat down on their pallet, and in the tiny space formed by their pack leaning against the wall, a pair of green sparks appeared for a moment, blinked as if unimpressed with the fuss, and then disappeared again.

For someone whose position was as precarious as Chih's, the proper response would have been to offer the kitten to the guard, or perhaps more passively, to put the kitten out the window.

Instead, Chih pulled the blanket up to their chin, turned to face the wall, and went to sleep.

Chapter Nine

In the morning, a brisk maid appeared with a tray of barley porridge and steaming corn tea for breakfast. Their room had turned clammy overnight, and Chih was glad to be out of it, eating instead on the edge of the walkway leading to the little listening room.

"So I heard some shouting about a white cat last night," Chih said casually.

The maid, happy to steal a moment and help Chih eat the pickled cucumbers that topped their porridge, nodded.

"Oh, the magistrate thinks they're unlucky," she said, and that was likely enough to be true. White was for mourning, and white banners were used by the imperial sanitation experts, marking out the boundaries of the famine for fear that its contagion might spread from county to county.

"I heard that they never ate the cats during the famine after the Oanh River flooded," Chih offered.

"They said it was because the cats were too fast, but it was really because one of the local guardian spirits kept hiding them under the ground. When the flood waters pulled back, they popped out of the ground like the first crop of water spinach."

"Oh, well, that's interesting," said the maid, finishing off Chih's pickles and neatly ignoring their bid for stories of her own. "Here, I'll run those plates back to the kitchen if you're done. If you like cats so much, you might like to go to the cats' graveyard by the west wall, beside the stand of cypresses. That's where all the family cats are buried."

Chih recalled that in this part of the country, there were distinctions made between family cats and the cats that were considered wild. Wild cats were the same whether they haunted the alleys in the capital or the rice paddies on the coast. They might be friendly cats that lived in the house or barn or granary, and they might be as gentle as a puff of cotton, but they were still not family cats.

Family cats were the purview of the wealthy and the scholarly elite. Their lines were kept as carefully as those of imperial dogs or horses, and their names repeated, leased from their ancestors like nobles leased their titles.

The cats' graveyard was a shaded place, dappled with sunlight with perhaps a half-dozen prayer tablets set into the ground for the Liu family cats. Chih wrote down their names, because eventually someone in the Singing Hills would want them, and then they paused at the one closest to the wall, shrouded in the deepest shadow.

DELICATE BLOSSOM, PRECIOUS COMPANION OF ORCHID.

They must have eaten the cat long before her mistress died, Chih thought. The cats of the Oanh River famine were protected, but few other animals ever received that kind of luck when a famine demon was about.

A whir of wings made them look up, and perched on the wall was a very welcome sight.

"Almost Brilliant! I was beginning to think you'd given up on me and flown home. Where have you been?"

The neixin had bathed her head in dust, making herself look as drab as any sparrow or nuthatch. She whistled two disdainful notes at Chih's greeting.

"As if you could get on without me. No. I was at the restaurant for a while yesterday, talking to Li Shui."

Chih snorted.

"While I might have been being killed or tortured? Thank you so much."

"I flew overhead to make sure you were all right. I saw you taking interviews and then taking dinner, so I judged that you were not doing so badly for yourself. *I* had to make do with a large stick insect."

"Such hardship for you, my good friend. Are you ready for some work?"

"I am always at work, as well you should know."

"Of course, my mistake. Listen, I need you to go to the graveyard across the river, high up on the hills. I want you to look for the grave of a woman, the accessory wife of Magistrate Liu. Her name was Deiyi, and she would have died during the famine."

Almost Brilliant whistled pertly.

"Why?"

Chih paused, because if they were honest, they weren't quite sure themself.

"Because. I suppose I want to see it was done right, that she had a place to rest."

Almost Brilliant studied them carefully, and seemed to come to some decision.

"All right, I shall. Be careful, though. They do not like you here. Shui told me that the Lius have no reputation for savagery or wickedness, but still you should be careful."

"They will be hospitable as long as I tell the story they want told," Chih said, and Almost Brilliant whistled with doubt.

"And how often do we do that?"

Almost Brilliant was winging her way into the sky before Chih had an answer to that, and Chih made their way back to the house.

Chapter Ten

Night came on fast, and with it came a strange and suffocating weight. There was a cold wetness in the air, and the lanterns seemed a poor protection from what waited beyond their flickering glow.

When Chih stepped out of the little listening room to stretch their legs, they shuddered. Their eyes went up to the trees first, where ghosts preferred to perch, but there was nothing there, no long hair hanging down like moss, no white skin gleaming like wet bone.

There was nothing to be seen, but that did not mean that they were safe. The place between their shoulder blades tingled as if something had set its eyes there, and when they caught a brief flash of motion out of the corner of their eye, they reeled back. Their hands came up to defend against whatever was coming, but it was only the maid who had brought them their breakfast.

They thought the girl would make fun of them, but she only gave them a sober nod.

"It feels terrible tonight," she said. "Come on. I'm meant to escort you to dinner, and it was bad enough walking here alone."

"It didn't feel like this before," Chih said.

"It always feels like this a little," the girl retorted. "But yes. This is bad."

They moved along the long walkway from the little listening room to the dining room. Chih was meant to be following the maid, but soon enough they were walking beside her, and then they realized their strides were growing longer and faster.

There was something in the darkness, something behind them and above them, and if they turned, if they turned—

By the time they gained the dining house, Chih and the maid were almost running, and they both pulled to a stop, red-faced and breathing hard.

"Did you feel—?" the maid began, and Chih nodded.

"Yes."

The maid composed herself, pulling on her briskness and efficiency like a shield.

"It's never too bad indoors. Go on in, you are expected."

Magistrate Liu knelt next to his wife at the low table, his tone high and irritated as he talked about an issue in the guardhouse. Madame Liu looked bored and tired, and that helped Chih calm their racing heart a little. Whatever was outside, it wasn't here with them, and they breathed a sigh of relief.

"We will eat dinner first," Magistrate Liu declared, "and after I will tell you about Zhan. Then, perhaps, you will understand Baolin."

Volumes had been written about Zhan and the famine there, but Chih nodded. It was another story that the magistrate wanted told, and listening was always free.

The fare was plainer than what had been served previously. The oil that made the vegetables and mushrooms so rich the night before was gone. Instead, plated on fine porcelain were domed scoops of plain brown noodles and vegetables steamed so lightly they were almost raw. There was no salt at all, no peppers, nothing that would allow the diners to believe they were eating for anything like pleasure. Chih found themself thinking wistfully of the pork at Li Shui's restaurant, where food might be a story, an inheritance, or a trick, but of course it would be delicious.

Dinner with the magistrate at the table was a silent affair. Madame Liu ate her food with a stolid determination that only hinted at how little she liked it. Magistrate Liu picked at the food with narrowed eyes, as if it were still too rich for his liking.

Finally, it was Magistrate Liu who broke the silence.

"Do the clerics of the Singing Hills remember the famine at Zhan?"

Chih looked up from their sparse meal, nodding.

"Yes, my lord. I have read some of those histories myself, but there are many records, written by both the ones who survived and the ones who did not."

"Then you understand," the magistrate said abruptly. There was, Chih thought, some kind of relief in his voice.

"As well as anyone who was not there might," Chih said cautiously.

Madame Liu shot them a narrow look, but Chih looked back, as bland as the food they were eating.

The magistrate examined the nearly unstained tips of his chopsticks for a few moments before setting them on the ceramic rest with a gentle chiming sound.

* * *

I was in Zhan as a fosterling in the house of my maternal uncle, Wang Dou. I was meant to study with him to gain some polish from the world before I returned to take my expected place in Baolin.

In those days, the land around Zhan was ceded for the national granary and for the billeting of the army. Instead of sprawling out, Zhan built up, until the towers, painted in dozens of shades of rose, jonquil, and teal, were visible from the watch stations on the Pearl Mountains to the head of the Stone Dragon of the west. The poor lived closest to the ground, waiting for the scraps that fell from above and climbing if they could as the attendants of the hydraulic elevators or the primitive pulley lifts which swung like mad from every level of the town.

In those days, Zhan was the favorite toy of the empire, and the flower and water district was called the clouds of the blessed. In the northernmost tower, there was the finest school for zither players in the empire of Anh, which is to say, the finest school for zither players in the entire world.

But of course you cannot eat sex. You cannot eat music.

Famine came to the city, in the form of rains that washed out all the crops and flooded the rivers so badly that no food could be brought in. Zhan's stores were large, but after forty days, they started to buckle, and after thirty more, they were gone. There was no way out with the water raging around us, and so we starved.

We could not eat sex or music, but of course we tried, and after that, we could not eat the madness either, that sent so many flying from the towers in a crazed hope for freedom. Some say that there were those who turned into birds and flew away, but of course that was nonsense.

We ate terrible things to survive. I am sure you know that. The paste that was used to fix our wallpaper to the walls, the taxidermied animals in the museums, the banners that we were so very proud of. We ate them all, and then when they were not enough, we turned upon each other. It began with a butcher from the clouds of the blessed, a secret dinner for the richest men in Zhan and their gaunt beauties, but it did not stay among the wealthy and the refined. Soon enough, we were told to let our beloved dead spoil in the damp, to rot for fear of worse desecration.

I never ate the flesh of others. I was tempted, more than once. My uncle offered himself up as he lay dying, hoping to sustain my aunt and my cousins for a little while longer. I refused to join their feast, nor the one that came later when my youngest cousin died.

I learned to eat dust, instead, and when I heard the great wings of the famine at Zhan, booming like an empty drum, I turned my face away. My aunt and my two cousins survived the famine. I imagine my cousins are in Zhan still, haunted the way the rest of the city was haunted, a wreck, a ruin, a monument to something once fine and then gnawed upon.

* * *

"And so I survived Zhan and returned to Baolin."

Chih did some quiet math. The famine at Zhan was some forty years ago. Magistrate Liu must have been a very young man if he wasn't a boy. To eat dust in

Zhan, to come back to fertile Baolin, what would that have felt like?

"And here you have ruled as magistrate since your own father died twenty-two years ago."

It had a ring of humble triumph to it, so the magistrate nodded and was satisfied.

"Just so," he said. "Just so."

As a man who had survived Zhan, Magistrate Liu was extraordinary. Everyone who had survived Zhan was extraordinary. So was everyone who hadn't survived it. There were small stories and strange stories and stories that were just outright lies, but the Singing Hills taught that there was no such thing as an insignificant story.

However, and it would have gotten Chih copy duty for a month if their teachers had heard them say it, extraordinary did not mean *special.*

Chih sneaked a glance at Madame Liu. The magistrate's wife was as still as a pond full of venomous carp, as perfectly composed as a painting of a murder.

Later, Chih thought.

There was a pair of boys with a lantern to light their way back to their room, and when Chih asked them if it was customary that there were two of them, they shook their heads. They left Chih with the guard before running off along the walkway, their feet thumping hollowly against the wood, and the guard looked like he might have liked to go with them.

Instead, he shook his head, crossing his arms over his chest and nodding towards their room.

"Go on in. I'll be out here."

It was on the tip of Chih's tongue to ask if he wanted to come in with them, but he took his seat across from the door, scowling as if he could scare the darkness away, and they went in.

The guard, as sullen as he was, was a comfort. They set their lantern aside, preparing for sleep, and as they did so, they listened to his breath, for the soft shuffle of his feet against the ground. The oppressive weight of the house hadn't let up at all, and now it felt like it was trying to come inside.

Before Chih lay down to sleep, they strung their cord of bells across the door. It was warded, designed to keep back all manner of ghosts and spirits, but as Chih plucked the cord and set the bells to chiming, it felt terribly insufficient.

The household had fallen into an uneasy calm, like a noodle shop where the owner was furious and everyone else walked soft-footed. The white kitten had found some other accommodations, and Chih was lonely without her. Without Almost Brilliant around, the kitten was a reminder that they weren't alone in the middle of all of this.

A few hours before dawn, Chih sat up suddenly on their pallet, unsure at first what had awakened them. Then they heard it again, a soft step on the walkway outside, a voice like the rattle of clean bones coming through the window.

"Come out. Come out. You must. I have ruled in Baolin for more than twenty years. Come out, little white one. I have fish for you. I have pork for you, if only you come out. Come out."

Oh, he thinks he's being perfectly reasonable, Chih thought blankly.

Magistrate Liu crossed the property two or three times more, rattling his fingernails on the wall to get the playful kitten's attention.

The kitten must have possessed at least an ounce of wit, because he never found her. Instead he walked up the paths and down them, waking Chih every time he went by, setting their heart racing with unease every time they heard his syrup-sweet rattling voice.

In the morning, Chih slid the door open and ducked under their belled cord. The dark circles under the guard's eyes matched their own. They exchanged a look and a shrug, and Chih went on to look for more stories.

Chapter Eleven

The morning sky was as clear and translucent as flint. There were no dark clouds in the sky, but Chih could feel something like a storm on the way, feel it between their eyes and in their chest. The people that they tried to speak to were more skittish, answering in single words or brushing them away entirely.

"Sorry. One of the household guards left without warning, and the magistrate is in a state," said the maid who had brought them their lunch. Her name was Yue, and she didn't have any stories she wanted to tell Chih.

"Not a good time to ask if I can go out to the village?"

"I wouldn't," Yue said with a shrug, and then she checked herself. "No, I would, and then I might not come back."

"That bad?"

Yue burst into tears.

It was over as soon as it began, and she looked mortified, shaking her head.

"Ugh, how humiliating. It's the pressure, I'm sure."

Chih considered her carefully.

"It's not."

"No. Not really."

Yue turned away, returning to her work with a vengeance. Chih had an unsuccessful talk with one of the guards, who started to say something interesting about a city to the far west that was drowned in snow, but then he was called away, and they were alone again.

At dinner, they gamely asked the magistrate and his wife if there was a chance they might go down to the town, see the sights, speak to some of the people. The magistrate, empty-eyed and distracted, had waved them away, *not yet,* or perhaps *not now.* His wife was silent.

Afterward, Chih ended up in the cats' graveyard, sitting among the tablets to take a few rubbings. Their stomach felt empty after another dinner of nearly raw vegetables, but they ignored it. A cool wind teased the back of their neck, and they looked up to see Almost Brilliant on the wall. The sight of her sent a rush of relief through them so profound they sobbed, and Almost Brilliant winged down to perch on their shoulder.

"No!" they cried, suddenly terrified. "Get out!"

She hooted with alarm, winging back up to the wall and gazing down at them with concern.

"Oh, you're not well, cleric."

Chih snuffled, wiping their eyes.

"No. I. I don't think I am."

"That's it. I'm making for the Sisterhood outpost. One of them can—"

Chih stifled another sob at the panic of Almost Brilliant leaving, at the thought of truly being alone.

"No. No. That is. Please don't. I'm just."

"Hurt? Imprisoned?"

"Afraid. I'm afraid. That's all. It's nothing."

"It's not nothing," Almost Brilliant retorted, but she settled down restlessly on the wall. "One more night. If things are still this bad tomorrow, I'm going to get you some help."

Chih swallowed, nodded. They could tolerate that better, Almost Brilliant leaving tomorrow night. Just not tonight. Not now.

"All right. Um. Sorry. Did you find anything at the graveyard?"

Almost Brilliant chirped scornfully at their less-than-subtle way of changing the subject, but she allowed it.

"No. No Deiyi, accessory wife to Magistrate Liu, not among the rich, or the poor or the unlucky."

Chih frowned.

"Deiyi was an accessory wife of the most important man in town. Even if she could not be buried in the family plots, she should have had a place somewhere.

They wouldn't have just left her for a mass grave. Did you look—"

Almost Brilliant shook her feathers irritably. "I looked everywhere. I went across the river, I went to all of the little family cemeteries, I went to the wall where they've written the names of the local saints, I went *everywhere.* She is not marked."

A deep chill settled in Chih's belly, heavy like a too-rich meal. They swallowed hard, wondering if they tasted dust on their lips, or well-water, or something that would allow them to live a little longer, and therefore delicious. They thought of the weight of a thick plate of bone and a length of rotting ribbon.

"Then. Then maybe she was up in the trees. Where we came down."

Almost Brilliant's voice was hushed, afraid.

"If that was her—"

Realization rose up through Chih's chest like a swelling tide. For a moment, it drowned them, over their head, covering their face, filling their mouth until it settled and they could almost breathe again and they turned to run.

"Cleric!"

"Get away from here," they cried. "I'll meet you at the restaurant tomorrow if I can. If I can't, go to the Sisterhood."

They ran, and as they ran, it came back to them, the feel of the rotted ribbon in their hands, the gleam of teeth in the soil. They had asked the Lady of the Thousand Hands for mercy, but what if it wasn't mercy that was wanted?

They came back to their room just as full dark fell. The lantern lit at the corner of the house swayed in the breeze, making the shadows dance. Inside, Chih regarded Hai who had arrived to watch over them with a lantern by his side. Instead of sitting across from their door, he stood as far away from it as he could, pacing the small space. He looked as if he wanted to faint with relief when Chih appeared.

"I'm glad you're here," Chih said.

"Why?"

In response, Chih took a deep breath and slid open the door to the room where they had been sleeping.

Where Deiyi had been watching them sleep.

She was visible now that Chih knew to look for her. The cord of bells swung, silent because her presence ate their sound, and she glared at them from lidless marbled eyes.

Green ribbons still hung from her braids, and her colorless robes were soaked with well-water, the dye washed out. Her hands came up, hooked into claws, and Chih realized with a sick turn of their stomach that someone needed to dig up the buried well, to find the guard who had disappeared.

Behind Chih, Hai drew in a thin and screechy breath of air, a sound that made Deiyi snap her eyes towards him. She studied him for a long moment and then looked back to Chih, coming to the limit described by the bells, and, to Chih's relief, no farther.

"I brought you back here," Chih said softly. "I'm sorry. I had no idea. I am so sorry . . ."

Deiyi's mute rage was palpable, but so too was her grief. It hung off of her like her sodden rags, and Chih's heart ached even as they thought of how they would describe this, from the ragged green ribbons to the long and elegant nails Deiyi had continued to grow after she died.

Chih started to recite a prayer, the one to the Lady of the Thousand Hands, the one almost everyone knew, but instead of growing still or calm, it only seemed to make Deiyi angrier. She paced back and forth like a lion behind the belled cord, shaking her head so hard that it sent old well-water splattering against Chih's lips.

Before Chih could finish the prayer, Deiyi came as close to the cord as she could, her eyes bugging out with fury.

"Look!" she said hoarsely. "Look!"

She opened her wet robes, fabric parting from flesh with a sucking sound and a smell like limestone and water rising up from her. It was too much for poor Hai, who uttered one last sickened cry and ran from the house entirely. Chih, for whom *look* was a foundational instruction, did, taking in the odd iridescence of the bare flesh in front of them, the slack belly and the empty breasts.

She showed Chih the place her daughter had been and was no longer, the places where she had starved to keep the little girl alive. Deiyi moved and raged and hurt, but she was dead, and it was a horror to see.

Something brushed by Chih's ankle, and when they looked down, the white kitten was beyond the barrier of the bells. For one terrible moment, Chih thought they were about to see the little animal ripped in half. Without thinking, Chih reached for the kitten, but Deiyi slashed at them, warning them back.

The kitten looked up at Deiyi for a moment, and then opened her mouth to cry out. The sound was sharp and piercing, and for the first time Chih realized how much it sounded like a child's insistent wail.

A moment later, there were thumping footsteps at the door to the hall, the magistrate's rattling shout, and then they knew.

Chih stepped forward, a warning on their lips, but the magistrate's ears were full of the kitten's cries. He thrust Chih aside, pushing them so hard they landed on their rear. Chih made another lunge for him, but he was moving fast. He crashed straight through the bells, and now they rang out, the sound clashing with the cries of the kitten, and the sound of wet cloth whipping around.

Then there was another sound, low, terrible, and *hungry,* and Chih's nerve and training broke. They scrambled for the door on all fours and then they found their feet with a breathy curse. There were people all about now, peering from the other buildings, some weeping, some with grim looks on their faces that told Chih that they knew more than they wanted to know, more than they had said.

Madame Liu came out in a lilac silk wrap that glimmered in the lantern light, clutching it closed to her throat. With her hair down and her face bare of makeup, she looked more vital than she had before, as sharp and as keen as the birds she had raised.

"You!" she said to Chih, and Chih shook their head.

"Get wards," they said. "Anything you can get, as long as it was blessed by someone holy. Get fire. I think once she's done with him, she'll just be done, but I wouldn't bet something important on it."

Madame Liu's hand came down on Chih's shoulder, digging her nails straight through the fabric to the flesh below.

"Who?"

"Deiyi."

The name made Madame Liu drop Chih's arm, her face going chalky white. She turned towards the screams coming from the hall, and Chih used the opportunity to get around her and head towards the gate. It was cowardly, perhaps, but they had seen Deiyi's eyes gleaming in the dark. She had stood over them as they slept. She hadn't killed them. Instead she had waited for the perfect night, the perfect bait, and Chih couldn't stand one more night in the house of Magistrate Liu.

There were no guards to stop them from leaving. They walked straight out, down the road they had walked up what felt like years ago. The walk back to Li Shui's restaurant felt as if it took forever. Every branch seemed to snag at their sleeves. Their toes seemed intent on finding every rock in the path. They fell two or three times in the dark, but they got back up and kept walking.

Shui was just taking the lantern down when they appeared, and they could tell how they looked in Shui's wide eyes.

"Are . . . are you all right?"

"No, not really," Chih said through chattering teeth. "Please. Can I stay? There's no trouble behind me, I swear, or at least if there is, it's only coming to me. I just need a place to spend the night."

Shui considered, and they realized how mad they sounded, how terrible they probably looked. They were prepared for Shui to turn them away, but instead he nodded, gesturing for them to follow.

He directed them to a narrow space with a pallet of buckwheat hulls and otherwise piled high with winter clothing, crates, and a fancy sign carved with the words RIVER QUEEN-LI'S BAOLIN PORK AND NOODLES!

Chih thought that Shui would retreat to his own bed, but he knocked on the door just a few short moments later with a mug of warm herbal tea and a small platter of cold chicken and noodles.

"Whatever has you looking like that, this probably won't hurt," he said firmly, and Chih started to laugh. They cut it off before Shui could get too alarmed, and they took the food from him with something like a smile.

"It will definitely not hurt," they said.

When the door closed behind Shui, there was a gentle scratching at the wooden shutter. A vision of Dei-yi's long nails came to them, but when the noise came again, along with a soft hoot, Chih rose to throw open the shutter and let Almost Brilliant inside. She flew swiftly to their shoulder, tugging at their earring and gripping so tight her claws pierced their robe straight through.

"Are you well? What happened?"

"I'm as fine as can be expected, just please don't make me talk about it before I've had some food."

They ate every scrap, and after they finished the last of the tea, they found themself steadier. Their hands stopped shaking, and when they pressed one over their heart, they found it beating at a near normal speed.

"All right, then." They looked around, and they sighed when they found Almost Brilliant, fluffed out until she was nearly spherical and roosting on top of the River Queen sign. If they moved close and listened hard, they could just barely make out the soft in and out of her sleeping breath. It had been a difficult few days for her too.

Chih stretched out on the buckwheat pallet, taking long deep breaths. In the silence, they could hear Shui across the hall, pages flicking as he thumbed through some book or pamphlet. He seemed too serious for the martial arts romances or the spy thrillers that had gotten so popular lately. It was probably a culinary manual of some kind, something about better ways to dress old meat or a catalog of spices and their properties.

Chih drifted off to the sound of pages turning, but when their eyes were closed, all they could see was Deiyi's body. All they could hear was her hoarse voice telling them to *look.*

Chih rolled up on the buckwheat pallet with a soft curse.

Fine.

They had looked, and now it was time to do what came after that.

The moon was up, full and bright. There was more than enough light for them to pull out their notebook and their graphite stub. The paper was as pale as a drowned woman's belly, the charcoal as dark as her hair, and Chih started to write.

Chapter Twelve

The next morning, Chih sat at a small table at the back of the restaurant, sipping on a mug of strong tea sweetened with a swirl of honey. Sunshine, Shui's cousin, sat next to them, carefully scratching out the characters for *pork, chicken,* and *fish* on her wax tablet.

"Show me some new characters?" Sunshine asked hopefully, and Chih blinked in surprise at being addressed at all.

"All right. Here, give me your hand."

They traced the strokes on Sunshine's palm with their finger before they realized what they had done, and then they watched the little girl faithfully reproduce the strokes on her tablet with a sharpened twig.

"There!"

"That's good," Chih said. "Next time, keep the stroke there shorter, and it'll be perfect. That. That says *hungry.*"

I want to go home, Chih thought.

There was a whir of feathers and then Almost Brilliant was sitting on the windowsill next to them, pushing her way past the shutter to hop onto the table. Sunshine squeaked with surprise, and Chih smiled with relief.

"I was wondering where you had gotten to," they said, and Almost Brilliant fluttered up to their shoulder.

"I went up to the magistrate's house."

Sunshine was looking a little too interested, so Chih took her tablet from her, scratching for a few moments.

"There. Why don't you go ask your cousin what that says?"

Sunshine ran off, and Almost Brilliant hooted curiously.

"When is she ever going to need the character for *dragon*?"

"You never know. What was going on at the magistrate's house?"

"A great deal of trouble, I should think. The gates were locked and guarded, and they had hung the banners for mourning."

"Did you see who they were mourning?"

"Who *should* they be mourning?" Almost Brilliant asked with a rather sharp glint in her eye.

"The magistrate, likely. At least one other, by rights."

With a weather eye out for little girls, Chih told Almost Brilliant what had happened the night before. A feeling of being both observer and observed came over them. They were now as much a part of this story as the Lius, Deiyi, and Orchid. It was discouraged for the clerics to become a part of their own accounts, but, as they had observed more than once, it was often inevitable.

Almost Brilliant tugged at their earrings, more thoughtful than reprimanding.

"It's not complete yet. Will you go back?"

"I likely shouldn't," Chih said. "I cannot imagine that I would be welcome."

"So what else is new?"

Before Chih could respond to that, the door to the restaurant opened, and Yue came in. She ignored Shui's greeting and came straight to Chih.

"You're wanted up at the house."

Chih considered her for a moment.

"Should I go?" Chih asked, and Yue blinked at being asked.

"I think you should. It was Madame Liu who sent me, and she has your gear packed up for you."

"She probably wouldn't do that if she wanted to dump me in the carp pond. All right."

* * *

The magistrate's house was cocooned in banners of white silk, and every flowering plant within the walls had been stripped of its blossoms. Chih felt dozens of eyes on them as they came back through the gates, but the eyes belonged to the living, and they did not mind.

Yue led them to a small room they had never been to before, small and swathed in yellow silk. There was a tray of tea and round cookies set on the low table, as well as a box desk for writing. As promised, their things were set neatly against the wall, waiting for them.

"Madame Liu requests that you make yourself comfortable and sit for a little while."

A calm settled over them. They had spent all of their fear and now the world looked bright and clear, as though through a clean glass. It would not last, but it was better than terror and wondering what had happened to the magistrate. They reached for a cookie with a shaking hand, but then there was a soft cough.

It was Madame Liu, in the little listening chamber, and the pipes carried her voice right to where Chih sat, as if she were just inches away.

Chapter Thirteen

My mother was so proud. She sent her daughter to be the wife of a magistrate in the south, and she sent her son to the imperial exams in the capital. My brother studied so hard he ended up hallucinating that our ancestors had come to chide him for his poor performance, but he did well enough.

We sat together on long summer evenings, and I listened to him practice answering sample questions from the exams that had come previously. It was terrible, because there were no answers to so many of those questions, because, I suppose, the inquisitorial board liked to see their prospectives grapple with the impossible. The last question I remember him answering was *what do demons eat?*

I listened to him recite cases from all over the world, trying to come up with an answer that no one had ever come up with before. Demons ate fat, hearts, livers, eyes, children, the last bite of every dish. They drank blood and tears and piss and rheum. They ate the clumps of hair that fall out when you don't eat enough fruit, and they drink the tears you can't cry because there hasn't been enough water. The answers are as numerous as hairs on a dog, and as unimportant.

In the end, they eat what you give up, what you can no longer keep back for yourself.

In the house of Magistrate Liu, we were lucky, and we knew that from the beginning. We were not lucky because we never heard the beating of the famine demon's wings, but instead because we only heard them softly. We thought that it was because we were rich, and there was something to that. The wealthy never starve as much as the poor do, no matter how bad things get.

One night, just a few weeks after Orchid died, I sat up in my bed while everyone else was sleeping. I had dreamed that there was one fat carp left, one whiskered fish hiding among the deepest rocks of the north pond. In my dream, she came up at night to nibble at the moonlight, and so she was full of silvery moon eggs.

I woke up drooling at how good those eggs would taste. Orchid was only a memory. My bones ached all the time, and it seemed as if I could never sleep enough, but still I found my way to the north pond. My wits were being nibbled away. I knew that the pond was empty even of the green moss and duckweed that grew there. There was no way a fish, however clever, could have hidden from us for this long. I told myself that over and over again, but I could not get the taste of moon eggs out of my mind or off my tongue.

I dipped my arm into the water over and over again, and over and over again, I came up with nothing but water. I sucked the water off my sleeve to get the faint flavor of cotton and weeds in my mouth, and finally defeated, I started back to my bed.

It was the hour of the cat, too long after sunset and too long until sunrise, and the entire house should have been shrouded in darkness. Instead there was a single light burning at the rear of the main hall, where my husband the magistrate meets privately with visitors of state.

The first thing I thought was that he had found something to eat, some fossilized plum, some scrap of chicken floss that he was preparing to eat with ritual, away from the eyes of those he was meant to shepherd.

I thought, *Perhaps he will share it with me.*

I thought, *Perhaps I can take it from him.*

I did not think that I would come close to the door of my husband's chambers and hear the voice of a demon.

"I have been patient. I am known for it. But I will not be patient any longer, Fei."

The voice of the demon scraped like talons across my mind, but it was no less chilling than hearing it wrapped around my husband's given name. I knew it from my marriage scroll, but I had never heard anyone call him by it, not in all the years we had been married.

"That isn't fair. It isn't fair. She must have been enough for you."

"Enough to fill some bellies. Enough to let your household live a little longer and feed me with their sorrow and their despair. I have fed off the grief of ten thousand in a single night, when the rice paddies at Kaifang were burned by one far greater than you. A grieving guilty household will only hold me for a little while longer, small man."

I saw their shapes against the paper shutter. I could see the wings of the famine folded up so it could fit into the room, monstrous and monstrously large. I saw my husband's shape as well, but though I half-expected it to be shifting, dog-headed or deer-headed, it was still that of a man.

"It is all I have," he said, his voice a whine. "She was my daughter, is that nothing? I have nothing left."

"That is not true. You live. You hold on to your pride. There are still things that will never cross your lips. If you will not give me more, I will take what I can get."

The magistrate groaned as if the demon had reached over to slit open his belly. Of course it had not. When every farm boy and falconer girl knows how to gut an animal before the blood spoils the meat, what would be the savor in that?

"Perhaps it is enough," the demon said courteously. "Famines end. Even if all of your household dies, perhaps you won't. You are wealthy. The rains will come and wash me away sooner or later."

"Always later, and the end is worse than everything that came before. In Zhan, the end was so much worse."

"And still you held back. That is what *I* remember. Then I made a meal of your resistance, the boy who sat back from his uncle's generosity to eat food made of dust. I ate that instead of the last shred of fat from your bones. I let you run all the way home to Baolin. What will you give me now?"

In the green shadows, I saw my husband's back bend like a shrimp's, curve so that his head nearly touched the ground.

"I will find something. Something rare for a famine. Something that will let me live a little longer."

Something delicious, I thought with a shudder.

I heard the rattle of talons on the wooden floor, and I pressed myself to the ground, my face against the sharp gravel. It was of the utmost importance, though I could not say why, that I not see the demon. Its wings boomed over my head, and I lay in the gravel by the walkway for a count of a thousand and then two thousand.

At some point, the lantern was extinguished, and I made my way back to the women's hall. Deiyi slept a drugged sleep as she had for days, and for once I was grateful for it. I missed her voice, I even missed her madness and her fury, but right now, I could bear nothing but silence.

I did not know what to do. I did not know what might come next. When I dreamed of Orchid, I dreamed of a laughing girl who could eat all she wanted, playing with the white kitten we had eaten two years before. She was beyond pain now, but none of us were, not even my husband the magistrate.

In the end, I was too tired to decide that night, and I closed my eyes. I slept a great deal in those days. We all did, when the hunger allowed us to.

We woke too early the next morning to hear that Deiyi had drowned herself. Her body poisoned that well so that we had to fill it in with rocks after, but still we would have eaten her, even if it would have made us sick to death.

Instead, my husband saw to it that her body was wrapped tightly in a gray cloth, only the loose green ribbons that tied up her hair trailing out. She was carried away, and we never saw her again.

Chapter Fourteen

Chih jumped when the door slid open and Madame Liu came in. Her eyes were as hollow as gourds, but there was firm line to her mouth, the resolution of a woman who had once done the unthinkable and then refused to forget about it.

She came and knelt across from Chih, the tray of cookies and now-cool tea between them.

"Well, cleric?" she asked. "Do you have the story you wanted?"

"He didn't eat her," Chih blurted out. "He didn't."

The pieces slid into place with a sickening finality, Deiyi's single word, *look*. Chih had looked, and Chih had seen what they were meant to see, though they had not understood it at the time. They had seen a body drowned, but intact. There were no knife marks, no torn flesh.

"Deiyi was drowned whole, cooked whole, and buried whole," Chih said, thinking of how smooth the bone they had carried in their pack had been. The records at Singing Hills called it pot polish, the slickness bones acquired when they had been cooked.

Madame Liu looked at Chih, wild-eyed as the pieces came together for her as well.

"Because he needed to give the Great Houshun something new, something it had never had before. Not eating a child in shame and darkness. Not killing a grieving woman."

"No, the Great Houshun has had plenty of both those things over the past few hundred years, I would think."

The demon had had worse, Chih knew. The clerics of Singing Hills knew what people would do when they were desperate enough, when they were hungry enough. At the famine of the Oanh River, the cats had been spared, but precious little else was.

"She told me to look," Chih said. "She wanted me to see the truth of it. Killed during a famine and not even . . ."

It was too brutal for Chih, but Madame Liu was made of something different.

"She was wasted," she said flatly. "And that is why my husband is dead."

They were both still, Madame Liu gazing at something that Chih couldn't see, Chih studying her face and committing the harsh lines of it to their memory.

"What happened to your husband?" Chih asked,

and Madame Liu turned her remorseless falcon eye on them.

"Have you not had enough of what has happened here? Have you not learned enough, *eaten* enough, of us?"

"Never." It was the truth, but an unwise one. Chih braced themselves for a tongue lashing or worse, but Madame Liu only lifted her chin, as disdainful as she would be over dealing with a merchant who would insist upon haggling.

"My husband is dead. Deiyi's remains will be buried with the proper honors and precautions. A very unwise and incautious cleric from the Singing Hills will be allowed to leave with what they have learned, and they will be content with that." She paused. "Have a cookie."

Chih choked on a laugh, the perfect hostess's encouragement in the field of horror, and they reached for one of the cookies without thinking of it.

It was light in their fingers, a design of buckwheat flowers stamped on the top. It was crumbly like almond cookies were and slightly grayish like rosemary cookies, but when they bit into it, it collapsed into a mouthful of dust.

Chih coughed, swallowing hard to get the dust off of their tongue. The clay cookie had been made with a sprinkle of salt on top. They could see where holding it in their mouth might make them think it was sweet, if they could bear dust in their mouth, if they could bear a hunger that demanded that it be swallowed at once.

"We still make them sometimes," Madame Liu said. "Pregnant women crave them, and of course there are some old-timers who will insist that they are good for you."

Chih finished the cookie with a careful second bite. It was terrible, coating their tongue with sludge. The idea of the dust mingling with their spit to make mud made them want to gag. They swallowed the second bite more quickly than the first, picking up the cup of cold tea to rinse out their mouth. It was, for a mercy, real tea, and they drank it down to the leaves. It tasted good, terribly good after the clay. It was easy to see how starving people might fight for that relief after three years of eating dust.

"Madame?"

"What more could you possibly want, cleric?"

"Only to know what you are going to eat tonight."

A number of emotions flickered across Madame Liu's face. Chih waited, and at last, a determined expression emerged. It was not happiness. Happiness might take longer to come if it came at all, but it was no longer repentance for a crime that was never wholly hers.

"I think I shall have pork."

Chapter Fifteen

Chih left Baolin the next day. Madame Liu had arranged a place for them with one of the trading outfits passing through to the coast, and from there, it would be an easy thing to pick up a ship going north. They could be back in the Singing Hills inside of two months, if all went well.

Before they left, they had a hasty breakfast with Shui and Sunshine, seated in the kitchen and with the sun just beginning to slide under the door. Shui stoked the oven with seasoned wood and made three bowls of buckwheat porridge topped with green scallions and slices of leftover ginger duck.

"It's road food for me for the next while," Chih said ruefully. "Thank you for giving me something good before that. Are you sure you won't take any payment for it?"

"For just this? I wouldn't be able to hold my head up if I did. My mother would be ashamed of me."

Chih thought of Shui's mother, who had fed the Great Houshun better than the richest man in Baolin could. They wondered if Shui would want to know that, if it would amuse him or make him feel strange in his own skin and his own town.

"You should come to the Singing Hills someday," they said by way of compromise. "It's a wonderful place, with copies of some of the greatest cookbooks in the world."

Shui laughed easily.

"And what would I do with them? All I really know how to do is cook pork. What a good thing it is that I know how to cook the best pork in the world."

"You might at that. Still, you should come."

"*I* am going to Singing Hills someday," Sunshine declared. "I am going to read everything they have about dragons."

Her wax tablet was covered with the character for *dragon.* Soon enough, Shui would have to hold it over a flame for her to smooth out the scratches and make it flat to inscribe again.

Chih pulled out their notes. In a few short months, they would be back at Singing Hills, copying their work into the cool catacombs where the records of hundreds of years waited. Magistrate Liu, Madame Liu, Deiyi, and Orchid would all be entered there, but it felt to Chih like that wasn't enough, or perhaps it was too much without something else to balance it. They flipped to a blank page and presented it and a stub of graphite to Sunshine.

"Here. Show me how well you can write *dragon.*"

As Sunshine labored over the character, Chih glanced at Shui.

"Last chance to have the famous Li family pork recipe filed with the roast swans and elixirs of immortality."

"Why should I? I already gave you the best of it in Mother's story."

A cough from Almost Brilliant got Chih moving, heading down the road towards the traders' camp. The neixin flew overhead for a short while, and then came to rest on Chih's shoulder, fluffing out her feathers, making herself comfortable.

Chih expected a scolding for carelessness or haste or any of the other innumerable ways they fell short as a cleric of the Singing Hills, but Almost Brilliant only cooed softly and sleepily, eyes half-lidded and sharp claws dug firmly into Chih's pack strap.

They found the traders easily enough, dark men and women from the highlands, more like Chih than the fair and slender people of the south. Chih fell into step with their wagon train, and around noon, instead of stopping for food, the traders kept on the march and passed around strips of soft dried meat. It had been pressed with fruit juice and chili paste, and it was impossible to tell what animal it had come from.

Acknowledgments

Okay, here's how you make a basic curry-style stew.

Heat a few tablespoons of oil in a large pot, and as it's heating, dice up an onion. Cook the onion in oil until it's soft, then throw in whatever flavorings you're into. I use curry powder, a splash of fish sauce or soy sauce (or both), garlic, maybe some extra cumin, maybe some MSG.

Before the onion burns, throw in your curry ingredients. If it's meat, you can be fancy and sear it in the aromatics before you throw in the rest, but you don't gotta. There's nothing wrong with a potato, carrot, and sweet potato curry. When everything's in, cover it with a cooking liquid. I like to use a combination of coconut milk and water.

Bring it up to a boil, then turn it down to a simmer.

Simmer until everything is cooked through, checking on it routinely. If it looks like it's going to boil dry, throw in some more water.

When everything's cooked, take it off the heat and let it rest for ten minutes before you serve it on the starch of your choice. It's always better the next day.

Thanks as always go to my agent, Diana Fox, who told me back in 2020 that maybe the world wasn't ready for famine and eating babies. Then in 2024, she said, "Okay, they may be ready now," and here we are.

For my editors at Tordotcom, Sanaa Ali-Virani and Stephanie Stein, thank you so much! Every time I don't fall flat on my face in a public and archival way, it's likely because of you.

For the Tordotcom team, who always has my back, thank you to Christine Foltzer, Greg Collins, Michael Dudding, Lauren Hougen, Amanda Hong, Kyle Avery, Jaime Herbeck, Jacqueline Huber-Rodriguez, Alexis Saarela, Sarah Weeks, Will Hinton, Claire Eddy, Lucille Rettino, and Devi Pillai.

Alyssa Winans continues to awe and delight with her covers, and Cindy Kay as the audiobook narrator is always so fantastic. Thank you so much!

Thank you to Cris Chingwa, Victoria Coy, Leah Kolman, and Meredy Shipp, here we are, and here we continue to be. That's not changing.

For Shane Hochstetler, Carolyn Mulroney, and Grace Palmer, you're always and forever the best, but this time an extra thank-you goes to Grace for checking the recipe above and making sure I didn't mess up.

Food's a lot of things. It's love, it's culture, and at the bottom of it all, it's survival. I hope you're getting the food that you need and the food that you like best. I hope you have enough to share. I hope you tell us all about it. I hope I see you next time.

About the Author

NGHI VO is the author of *Siren Queen, The Chosen and the Beautiful, Don't Sleep with the Dead,* and *The City in Glass,* as well as the acclaimed novellas of the Singing Hills Cycle, which began with *The Empress of Salt and Fortune.* Her work has been nominated for the Nebula, Locus, and Lambda Literary Awards and the Los Angeles Times and Ursula K. Le Guin Prizes, and has won the Crawford, Ignyte, World Fantasy, and Hugo Awards. Born in Illinois, she now lives on the shores of Lake Michigan. She believes in the ritual of lipstick, the power of stories, and the right to change your mind.

nghivo.com
nghivo.bsky.social